EZAKIEL ADVENTURE
TO ENCHANTED FOREST

EZAKIEL ADVENTURE
TO ENCHANTED FOREST

ANN

Ezakiel Adventure To Enchanted Forest

Copyright © 2020 by Ann Ally. All rights reserved.

No part of this publication may be reproduced, stored in a retrieval system or transmitted in any way by any means, electronic, mechanical, photocopy, recording or otherwise without the prior permission of the author except as provided by USA copyright law.

This novel is a work of fiction. Names, descriptions, entities, and incidents included in the story are products of the author's imagination. Any resemblance to actual persons, events, and entities is entirely coincidental.

The opinions expressed by the author are not necessarily those of URLink Print and Media.

1603 Capitol Ave., Suite 310 Cheyenne, Wyoming USA 82001
1-888-980-6523 | admin@urlinkpublishing.com

URLink Print and Media is committed to excellence in the publishing industry.

Book design copyright © 2020 by URLink Print and Media. All rights reserved.

Published in the United States of America
ISBN 978-1-64753-446-2 (Paperback)
ISBN 978-1-64753-445-5 (Digital)

01.05.20

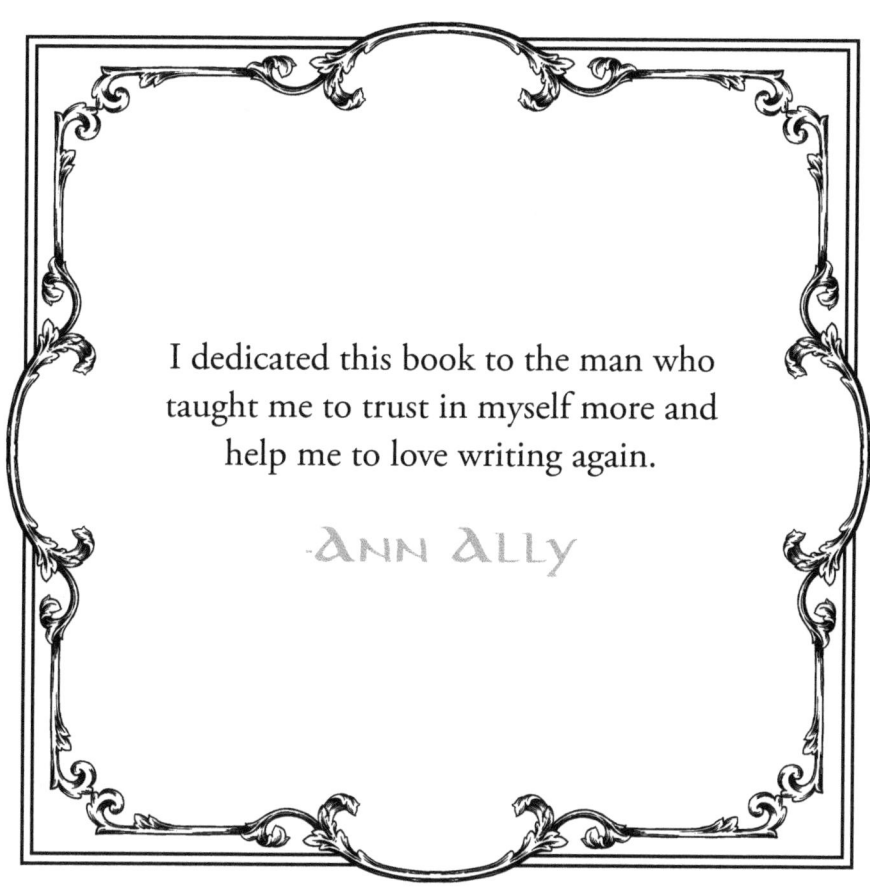

I dedicated this book to the man who taught me to trust in myself more and help me to love writing again.

-Ann Ally

In a faraway kingdom, there was a land hidden in a valley between two vast mountains. The mountains stood like walls, preventing any dark power from approaching in the east. The land was covered with fresh, green grass and many different kinds of wildflowers.

The kingdom was known as the Land of Gardenia. Before the kingdom was built, Queen Rose lived with her uncle, the ruthless King of Apalonia. She did not like the way her uncle treated his people with no mercy, so she decided to walk away from him along with his people who were willing to follow her to build a new home. Her uncle did not stop her, for he believed that someday Queen Rose would return to him.

However, with her patience and determination, she managed to build a kingdom where her people lived in peace and harmony.

Her willingness to go through hardship for her people made her deeply loved and treasured by the people of Gardenia who, out of love, built a garden in the middle of their small town with her name carved on the stone.

After five years, Kingdom of Gardenia had finally built their own army, trained their own soldiers and knights to protect their land. Queen Rose had made an acquaintance with other kingdoms such as Margold and Vnox. With their alliances, her kingdom could be protected from unwanted enemies. Every day, farmers, shepherds and fisherman would go to town and bring all their goods to be put it in the granaries. It was easier to keep their food stock in one place. Unlike her uncle, Queen Rose charged lower taxes so the people could afford to pay. The people did not feel burdened with their lives here in this kingdom because of her kindness.

When the spring came, the residents celebrated the Flower Festival with Queen Rose. Everyone worked together to decorate their gates and fences around their village and cover them with wild flowers from their valley. It symbolized their land and the peace and harmony among their people. At night, the people would attend a ball that was held by Queen Rose in the castle hall. Everyone would come and they would usually dress up beautifully for the party. Their night would be filled with endless joy, music and cracking fireworks.

Ezakiel Adventure To Enchanted Forest

But one day, Queen Rose fell terribly ill. Her body was weak and she could barely eat or drink. A physician said that her sickness was caused by a curse; he knew Queen Rose's uncle had put it on her by the help from a witch. The physician heard the news when he came to King Arganold's kingdom to treat one of his soldiers.

She did not want to tell her people because she knew that they would worry for her health. So she told Ezakiel not to tell anyone. Ezakiel was one of her noble knights; he always put himself first to protect the Kingdom. She adored the young lad like a brother.

"Your majesty." He bowed down.

"Ezakiel…come." She gestured for him to come closer, her voice was hoarse and she could only speak slowly.

When Ezakiel reached for her hands, they were cold and he tried to hold back the tears. Queen Rose had been kind to him and she did not deserve to be in this state.

"There must be a cure for this, your majesty." Queen Rose smiled upon hearing his remarks.

"If such cure existed, would you find it for me?"

"Yes, no matter how long it would take." Seeing the determination in his eyes, the sorrow in her heart lifted up.

"My mother once told me about the myth of the Forbidden Rose; it can cure anything from wounds, illness and even has the power to bring death to life. She said there is a keeper, a fairy, every riddle that she gives, might lead you to have it but if you answer it wrongly, then the rose would be forever gone." Ezakiel had heard about this Forbidden Rose when he was little.

"But it is only a myth your majesty, we don't even know where to search for it."

"It is not a myth, Ezakiel. My uncle had once sent his knights to bring him the flower, and the witch told him to start their quest in the dark forest. But a few days later, my uncle received news that his knights had died after they had been attacked by vicious wolves. "

"You mean the dark forest is the key to find the Forbidden Rose?"

"Yes, the rose must not fall into the wrong hands. That is why searching for it won't be easy."

"What if the witch was lying about the whereabouts of this rose?" She tightened her grasp on Ezakiel's hands.

"The witch would never lie. She was my friend before my evil uncle ordered for her to be burned alive because of the knights that he had lost." Ezakiel felt guilty upon hearing this.

"I will not push you, Ezakiel. But if you want to search for my cure, you must go alone. The more men you bring into the forest, the more lives will be lost. The forest knows when it feels threatened." He understands that to be in the dark forest, you must come with a good heart. If it senses danger, then the creatures in the forest would attack you day and night.

"Your wish is my command. I will not let you suffer from the curse. The people need you and so does the kingdom." Queen Rose drifted off to sleep with a smile on her face. She knew that Ezakiel was a brave warrior and might be a great leader someday.

The next morning, Ezakiel rode his horse, Saggy, straight into the dark forest. When he approached the forest, the weather was cloudy and the air was cold. He tries to hold his worry at bay. Ezakiel did not know where to begin his quest. He could only see trees everywhere, so when he saw a trail of smoke appear above the trees not far in the distance, he decided to move towards it.

As he got closer, Ezakiel realized that the smoke was coming from a cottage. He dismounted his horse and knocked on the door gently. He could hear something moving around inside—then a lady with red hair appeared in the doorway.

"Who are you?" She asked with her hand on her waist.

"Ezakiel, Knight of Gardenia." There were glints of recognition in her eyes when he mentioned Gardenia. She must have known where Gardenia was.

"What would a knight of Gardenia do in the dark forest? Especially here?"

"I need your help. You seem to know more about this place than I do."

"Quite right!" She said it with pride. Indeed she was a woman but this forest had been her place since she was little.

"My queen has been cursed and she believes the only thing that can cure her is the Forbidden Rose. I don't know where to search for it. The only clue that I have is in this dark forest."

She tapped her feet and bit the inside of her cheek.

Ann

"Come inside, I will tell you what I know." Ezakiel was happy to hear that. He stepped inside as soon the door was held open for him.

His eyes roamed the inside of the cottage. It looked clean and tidy, there were some swords, bows and arrows hung on the wall. The smell of some brewing soup that had been cooked made his stomach growling.

"I'm Belinda, here, have some of this. It would keep your body warm." Ezakiel sat in the chair that had been set in the middle of the room. She gave him ale that tasted so strong, it made him cough after one swallow.

"Is it just you living here?" He wiped his mouth with the back of his hand and tried to sound casually after drinking the ale. It burned his throat.

"I live with a shaman and his wife. I'm an orphan. They have taken care of me like I were theirs."

"Why here? This forest is dangerous." Belinda took a sit opposite of him with both of her hands were on top of the table.

"It is not so dangerous if you're not a threat. I like it here, the nature, and the breeze. This place is just perfect." Ezakiel found himself smiling at this strange woman. Most of the women he had met had been delicate and graceful, but with her, he only saw an adventurous woman.

"Do you know where the Forbidden Rose is?" She paused for a moment.

"I do."

"Where is it?" He asked nicely.

"Not here obviously," She tried to make a humor out of it. It was not often she got the chance to speak with strangers, let alone a knight. "You need to enter a portal to another realm where the Rose is kept hidden." Belinda got up and walked to a shelf and searched for something. She opened a box that was loaded with scrolls; she clapped in delight when she took one scroll out of the box. She spread it on top of the table and Ezakiel looked at it in great puzzlement.

"What is this?" He asked.

"A key to open the portal. My father always used this to get into the enchanted forest for herbs."

"How did he get this?"

"I don't know. It was passed down to him by his ancestors. Now, please be silent, I'm trying to concentrate."

Ezakiel did not say a word after that; she was reading the foreign language that was written on the scroll. When she closed her eyes and spoke the language, Ezakiel felt like his body was going back and forth. The energy inside the cottage became too strong; it made his head feel dizzy. He did not know what was happening but he saw the forest outside spinning around – or perhaps the cottage was.

"What's going on?" Ezakiel had to ask when Belinda had finally stopped chanting the words.

"I just made us a portal," He stared at her in blank expression. "Now sir knight, I must warn you, not many creatures in this enchanted forest are good. We may confront mystical creatures that could eat us alive." Ezakiel made the same expression when she said mystical creatures.

"Are we in the enchanted forest already?" He asked.

She nodded vigorously.

"Now let's go find your Forbidden Rose." Belinda stood and tied her robe and dagger around her waist. Ezakiel shook his head in disbelief.

"You're not coming with me, are you?" She smiled.

"I bring you to this place so I must come. You never even have been into the enchanted forest." He could only sigh in defeat. Belinda is one headstrong woman that would not say '*no*' to him.

"Fine, but stay close to me." Belinda finally laughed and said, "You're the one who should stay close to me."

When they stepped out of the cottage, Ezakiel realized that Saggy was not there and what stood in front of him was a forest full with large trees that almost looked like gigantic canopies. In the dark forest it was dead silent but here he heard sounds of birds chirping as if welcoming him into the enchanted forest. The grass was far greener than that of his land in Gardenia; even the flowers filled the air with their intoxicating smells.

ANN

Ezakiel had never been to this place and he had never believed that such place could exist. Belinda already walked in front of him. He had to keep up with her and it looked like he had no choice but to follow.

"How do you know that the Forbidden Rose is in here? How do you know about this forest?" Those questions poured out of his mouth like rain. Belinda threw a side glance at him. "You really do ask a lot of question. But to answer your questions, I know about this forest because my father found me here when I was a baby. The last time I came here was with my father to find herbs that grew in this forest. I heard Gloria talk about the Forbidden Rose. I don't know in which part of this forest that the Rose is hidden though. I only heard story from her."

"Gloria? Is she a mystical creature?" He couldn't believe what he was hearing right now.

Belinda nodded. "Didn't I warn you about the mystical creatures that live here?"

"Yes…but I find it hard to believe." She stopped by a river. The water was as blue as the sky above.

"Well, you will believe after you see this." Belinda pointed towards the rocks near the waterfall.

Ezakiel froze on his spot when he came face to face with mermaids that were always told in fairy tales.

"Are those …"

"They are the waterfall mermaids; they like to play near the rocks. No need to be worried, they are harmless." Belinda whistled and all heads turn to her.

Those mermaids had such beautiful long and wavy hair. They accessorized their hair with flowers and shells that they found in the sea. Their tails were in different colors, some of them were green, blue and gold. Their scales could glimmer like diamonds under the sun. Belinda liked it when the mermaids sang, it sounded so beautiful. The last time she saw them was when her father brought her here.

A mermaid with a gold tail saw Belinda with him and swam towards them. She popped to the surface and sprinkled at them with water. Belinda stepped back instantly.

"What brings you here?" That question was for Ezakiel and he looked at Belinda who tried to shake off the water on her dress.

"I'm searching for the Forbidden Rose for my Queen. Do you know where I can find it?" He asked.

"I can but I need something in return." Belinda snorted beside him.

"Gazebelle is one of the mermaids who likes shiny things. Give her one and she may want to tell you where to find it." The mermaid smiled at her while flapping her tail in the water. Belinda was almost soaked because of it and she groaned in distress.

Ezakiel reached for his sword that Belinda had pointed to be used as a trade in order to get information from this young mermaid. A knight never went to a quest without his swords but when he looked at the dagger that still locked around Belinda's waist, he felt slightly relieved that they still had a weapon.

"Have this…" The mermaid reached for it and caressed the steel sword in amazement.

"It's beautiful." She said in a whisper. "The information, please." Belinda insisted.

"Be patient my dear, I keep my promises," Gazabelle put the sword in the bubble that she made with water and made it afloat behind her.

"Just follow this path; it will lead you straight to the place where you want to be. But beware, once you have found the cave, there will be a dragon waiting for you. The gate to the garden is on the cave walls, you must search for it, fast, before the dragon wakes up." Ezakiel saw Belinda's nervousness.

"Thank you. I'm grateful for your help." The mermaid waved at them and returned to the other mermaids with the prize that she had obtained from Ezakiel.

"You can go back home, Belinda. Let me do this alone." She smirked at him.

"Me? going home while you are stranded here? No, I will not. I will follow you until you have found the Forbidden Rose." Belinda walked on the path that led them deeper into the forest. The blue flowers along the path made it easier for them not to take different direction from what they had been pointed.

While walking, Ezakiel tried to make a conversation with Belinda. He wanted to know her better. He had this urge to unravel the mystery of her past.

"If your father found you here, doesn't that mean you probably could have been a daughter to a mystical creature that lived here in this enchanted forest?" She shrugged.

"I don't know. I never feel like one of them, I just feel like me, human."

"Have you tried searching for your real parents?" She slowed down to walk side by side with him.

"I have but it has been in vain." Ezakiel frowned.

"They must have left you with something, to remind you of them." Belinda's hands suddenly moved to unclasp the necklace around her neck.

Ezakiel did not notice it when he first met her - until now.

"Only this, with my name written on it." She handed it to Ezakiel for him to see. The pendant was a small rode crystal. There's something written on it other than Belinda's name. He stared at it thoroughly.

"Forever and always." He said.

"What?" Belinda wanted to take a closer look at the words that he had read, and could not believe that she had never noticed those words before.

Before she could grab the necklace from him, the pendant suddenly glowed brightly. Belinda was both surprised and petrified. "What did you do?" She asked him.

"I didn't do anything, but look; the light is pointing towards that land over there." Their eyes followed the light that was pointing towards the left side of their path.

"We should go; I have the feeling that what you are looking for is right there." Ezakiel grabbed her by the hand

and started dragging her to the left. Belinda stopped him and said, "I'm here to help you, we came here for the Rose."

Ezakiel could sense that Belinda was afraid to confront what was ahead. He did not blame her; she had never seen her family since she was a baby. The truth could be scary and most of the time, hurtful.

"It is the least that I can do for you for bringing me here, Belinda." Without waiting for her reply, Ezakiel took the lead and held her hand in encouragement.

The light led them to an abandoned castle. Both of them were in awe when they stepped inside; the walls were made of crystals, the floor was visible for them to see the blue water that was flowing below. The hall was twice bigger than the one he had seen in Queen Rose's castle and what amazed him was the throne that stood before them.

"Do you think that my parents would be here?" Belinda looked at him; hope was in her eyes.

"I don't know but we will find out." The pendant had stopped glowing and they were now on their own to find out the connection of this place with Belinda.

They walked around to find something that could tell what the place once had been. Ezakiel told Belinda not to go far; he did not have his swords with him. Having Belinda by his side would keep them out of danger.

"Have you found anything?" He raised his voice loud enough for her to hear.

"No, just an old painting." What Belinda found was actually a painting of a king and a queen, sitting on the throne at her side. The man had a look of an elf. However, his queen was human, just like her and Ezakiel.

She yelped in surprise when a goblin tugged at her dress. The goblin was short and he had pointy ears and sharp teeth that could effortlessly slice meat. Belinda screamed when it smiled.

"Please don't scream." The goblin looked alarmed by the reaction the he got from her. He only wanted to meet these people who had come into this castle.

Ezakiel heard her scream and quickly ran to get her. When he saw the goblin, Ezakiel instantly pulled Belinda behind him.

"Stay away from us, creature." He said.

"I'm sorry; I didn't mean to scare her." When the goblin moved closer, they took a step back. "I'm not going to hurt you, I promise." He put his hands up.

"Who are you?" Ezakiel asked and tried to stay calm, when the creature distanced himself from them.

"I'm Giddy and you are…?"

"Ezakiel and Belinda." Giddy looked at the woman behind Ezakiel. Something familiar about her face, he tried to remember where she had seen her.

"Why are you here?" Giddy frowned at them and Belinda felt at ease when the goblin did not look like it was going to hurt them.

"Belinda's necklace led us here; I believe that we could at least find her long-lost family." Ezakiel showed Giddy the necklace that he had gotten from her. When the little goblin took it, he slowly moved towards the painting that Belinda had discovered. Giddy did not reply to his remarks, he was too busy staring at the painting and the necklace.

"This place, it is abandoned right? Do you know who used to live here before?" This castle was magnificent. Why would someone leave this place? Ezakiel wanted to know to fulfill his curiosity. Belinda's parents might have been among the people who used to live here.

"It used to be the castle for King Elve's and his Queen Belinda Cronotia," His remark caught Belinda by surprised. They both have the same name. "I used to serve them as a messenger in this castle; they both loved by the mystical creatures here but not the Dark Elf, the king's brother. He was jealous to see the king loved by his people and have

Belinda Cronotia as his Queen. When the queen gave birth to a human princess, the Dark Elf met his brother and put a crystal sword into his heart." Giddy looked down in sadness. The memory still brought sorrow to him.

"I was with the Queen at that time and she asked me to take her child away from this place," Ezakiel looked at Belinda who was silent while listening to his story. "I couldn't say no, she was crying, I didn't want to do it, but if the child stayed in the castle, the Dark Elf would have harmed her. I knew it because the castle was under attack by the Dark Elf's soldiers."

He turned to face both of them. The necklace was dangling from Giddy's hand.

"I run deep into the forest until I came across a man who was picking herbs in the forest. I was scared that the Dark Elf would find me and take the baby, so I just left the child for the man to find. I knew the man was not evil, if he was, I would have sensed it. The moment he picked the child, I run back to the castle only to see that there were nothing left but dead bodies on the floor."

"What about the Queen?" Belinda finally broke her silence; something made her feel sad with the story. Deep down in her heart, she knew there was a possibility that the child could have been her.

"I found her dead in bed…I yelled out her name, but the Queen would not wake up," One little tear escaped the corner of his eyes. Ezakiel realized that although the goblin looked scary, but his heart was pure and kind.

"This necklace was supposed to be the gift that she left for her daughter. Where did you get this?"

"It's mine," Belinda knelt down to face the goblin. "My father found me in the forest while he was collecting herbs. He brought me to the human world; he kept me safe and raised me as their own child."

The goblin looked at the painting and back to her. He realized that the color of their hair was the same with the Queen. He even remembered that these two strangers came here to find her long-lost family. Giddy knew that this was not a coincidence.

"If this necklace is yours, then you must be the…child to King and Queen Belinda, the child that I ran off with during the attack."

She wanted to deny that, but, what she had seen and heard was precisely similar with what his father had told her. It brought tears to her eyes. With the help of Ezakiel and this little goblin; she finally found her real family. Belinda hugged the goblin tightly.

"It is you, my princess, my dear princess…" Giddy wiped the tears from her face and put the necklace around her neck. When she had put it back on, Giddy saw the Queen that he always adored.

"I found my family, Ezakiel! I found my family!" She exclaimed in pure happiness while looking at the painting.

"I'm glad." He said.

"I buried your mother and father in the pixies field. Do you want to come and see their graves?" Though it broke her heart to know that her parents had been killed, to see their burial site would end her longing for them.

"Yes." The day was still bright and Ezakiel wanted Belinda to see her family, so he put his own quest to a temporary halt for her.

Giddy brought them far away from the castle into a field that was filled with dandelion flowers. Once they were there, Giddy whistled with both of his hands at the corner of his lips to wake the pixies. Belinda covered her mouth in amazement and looked fascinated when all the pixies flew up in the air to greet them. The pixies were bigger than her thumb, their wings looked like fireflies but the pixies themselves looked almost like the flowers.

Giddy whispered to the pixies that he had found the lost princess and they let out a small gasp while looking at each other. Belinda giggled at their reaction.

The pixies came to her, flying around her until Ezakiel could not see Belinda between those fairies.

"What are they doing to her?" He asked.

Giddy who was right by his side, smiled at him.

"To turn her into a princess." As soon the little goblin said it, the pixies stopped swarming around Belinda. She looked down on herself and was surprised to see that her dress had turned to white and the crown that they had put on top of her head really made her look like a princess. The dagger was still secured around her waist and she felt relieved that they did not take it off.

"You look beautiful." Ezakiel felt something bloom inside his heart with her transformation. He vowed that he would never forget the smile on her face.

"Thank you." Belinda was embarrassed to be complimented by him, but she appreciated that he did.

"Come princess, it's time to meet your parents." Giddy walked forward and both of them followed from behind.

The pixies were still flying on top of their heads; it was like watching the snows from outside the window.

"This is the place." Giddy stopped in front of two tombstones. She knelt down and touched the stones with her heart full of love. She never thought that this day could be the best day of her life. Her parents would be always remembered in her heart, she would never forget the sacrifice that they had made to keep her alive.

"Papa, mama...I love you." Ezakiel who heard this, knelt beside her and tried to comfort Belinda with a hug.

He was grateful for leading her here. She was a strong princess in his eyes.

While they gave Belinda a moment to be with her family, Giddy and Ezakiel sat on the grass while watching the pixies play with each other.

"What happened to the Dark Elf after that?" He asked; wanting to know more about Belinda's past.

"He died in the war with gargoyles. Most of the mystical creatures chose to live on their own soon after that. I choose to stay near the castle; my heart aches when I am away from this land." Giddy was a faithful servant to his king and queen, if they were alive right now, they would be proud of him.

"Do humans always come to this place?" Ezakiel wondered.

"No, some have the key to this place and some accidently find it. Her mother was lost here until she met the king and she immediately fell in love with him." Ezakiel found out about the happy life her parents had had before the Dark Elf decided to kill them.

"How about you? What are you doing here?" Giddy looked at him who kept on staring at Belinda.

"I'm here looking for the Forbidden Rose to heal my Queen. She has been cursed by her uncle. I need to find the Rose for her." Giddy was alarmed upon hearing his remarks.

"You must be brave; the rose is protected by a butterfly fairy, she never likes someone to enter her garden, especially if you come to search for the Rose. She even has a dragon to guard the entrance to her garden." It surprised Ezakiel that Giddy knew more about the place that they wanted to go. Giddy remembered that place because he used to send a message to the butterfly fairy by the order of his king.

"I must try, there's no point of giving up hope after we have come this far." Belinda came close to them and heard their conversation. She felt bad for delaying him on his quest to find the Rose for his Queen.

"We must go. Thank you for bringing me here Giddy and thank you for saving me." She planted a kiss on his cheek and Giddy could see that the princess had grown into a beautiful woman.

I'll help you to go there. It's the least I can do for both of you," he called out the pixies and once again they swarmed around them in circle. "What are they doing?" Ezakiel asked Giddy.

"Pixies can transport us to your destination. Just close your eyes." As soon as he said it, they both did as they were told. They could feel being lifted up but they did not have the guts to open their eyes to see, scared that they might be being flown high off the ground – which indeed what the pixies were doing.

It took them two minutes until they felt that they had landed on the ground. Ezakiel and Belinda who had never flown before felt slightly dizzy as soon as the pixies had flown off and left them in a strange place.

Giddy, who saw their pale faces, burst into a laugh. He found it very amusing.

"Is this the place?" Ezakiel asked him after he regained his composure.

"Not quite, that's the place you will be going to." He said, pointing towards a cave in the mountain. Belinda suddenly felt nervous and scared, she thought this quest could be easy, but it was certainly not. She knew about the dragon that would be inside the cave. They had nothing but a dagger.

"The dragon likes to keep treasures in his cave. If you meet him, try not to wake him up. At this hour, the dragon might be sleeping just like the last time when I was here. Enter the gate to the garden as quickly as you can, there is only one gate there, so it won't be hard for you to find it." Ezakiel tried to memorized everything that Giddy had told him. It might come in handy once they were inside.

"Thank you Giddy, you've been very helpful." Giddy did not want to enter the cave with them. He had the feeling that it would be much better if they did it without his help. So he just watched them walk slowly towards the cave.

Before they disappeared into the darkness, Giddy called out Ezakiel's name. He turned to face the goblin.

"Take care of the princess for me." Ezakiel smiled and nodded in agreement.

Belinda used her necklace to guide them in the darkness. Somehow her necklace had suddenly lightened up when they went deeper into the cave. She did not know how it happened but she was grateful that they could watch their steps in this cave. Ezakiel was walking behind her; they both looked at the walls of the cave that were filled with treasures and gold.

There were so many coins on the floor, when they stepped on them, the coins made a clicking sound that could awake the entire cave. However, Belinda saw something that caught her eyes; a necklace that was filled with rubies, dangling around a majestic goblet; it was so beautiful that she was subconsciously walking towards it.

Ezakiel frowned at her, he followed her gaze and when he saw the necklace, Ezakiel just shook his head. Belinda might have been a tough woman but accessories would always be a woman's friends. Queen Rose had the same expression whenever she laid eyes on fancy jewels.

Belinda's hands reached for it and she could not wipe the smile away.

She loved the necklace so much and she was sure her mother would too.

"It's beautiful." She said in a whisper. "Yes it is." Ezakiel came beside her to inspect the necklace.

"I would love to give this to my mother once we go back home. She would celebrate her birthday tomorrow. " And Belinda planned to make a big cake for her.

"But this treasure is not ours; this necklace belongs to the cave. We shouldn't take it." Ezakiel was right; she would be considered stealing if she took the necklace. So Belinda put it back with a heavy heart.

"You're right, I'm sorry."

"Don't be," Ezakiel lifted her chin so she could stare into his eyes. "I make you a deal. When we are back to our place, I will give you some of my things as presents for your mother." He tried to bring the smile on her face. He liked the radiance of her beauty when she was happy.

"Alright then." Belinda agreed and they continued walking in the cave.

The deeper they went, the more gold and treasure chests they found inside. They tried to be quiet as they went deeper into the cave.

Ezakiel stopped dead in his tracks when he felt a warm wind blowing at his side. His hair was pushed to the right because of the wind. Belinda turned around to see Ezakiel, but, what she saw was him standing closer to a sleeping dragon. They did not realize that they finally had come closer to the gate and the dragon itself.

Belinda panicked when the dragon moved slightly, they both hold their breath.

Ezakiel waved his hand for her to hide behind the rock that was not far away from her. She hesitated at first; she would not leave Ezakiel to deal with the dragon by himself. But, Ezakiel insist and she do as she was told.

She tiptoed to hide behind the rock. She crouched silently behind it but her feet suddenly kicked a treasure chest that was filled with gold coins and jewels. Those coins had somehow fallen onto the floor and made clinking noise that hurt her ears.

She bit the inside of her lips and popped her head out to see if the dragon had been awakened by the noise.

The dragon saw Ezakiel and rose up with both of its wings spread open. The dragon had a scale like it was made of steel, four of its legs looked like a frog with razor blade claws. Ezakiel had no chance of fighting this dragon.

Ezakiel Adventure To Enchanted Forest

Ezakiel just stood there motionless. The dragon bared his teeth.

"Who dares to enter my cave?" His voice echoed around the cave, Belinda stayed hidden while keeping an eye on Ezakiel.

"I'm Ezakiel, your noble dragon." Ezakiel bowed down at the dragon and tried to charm his way out of the mess. He wanted the dragon to know that he was not a threat.

"What are you doing here? Are you trying to steal my treasures?" The dragon suddenly became angry; his spiky tail waved from side to side, anyone who got hit by it could end up dead. "No, we want to enter the gate," said Ezakiel who suddenly spotted a gate behind the dragon. He felt relieved that he had finally found his destination. Soon Queen Rose could rule the kingdom once again.

"I can't let you enter the garden unless you give me what I fancy the most." Belinda who heard that had something in mind. She looked at the treasure chest in front of her. Giddy had said that the dragon loved gold and treasures. This cave was full of them. The dragon would not know that the treasure chest had been here in the first place. She needed to use the chest so that they could enter the garden without fighting the mighty dragon.

Belinda showed herself to the dragon with the treasure chest in her hands. It was heavy but she used to carry heavy things while helping her father in the woods.

"We can give you our gold." Ezakiel looked stunned by her bold move but when he looked at the dragon, he saw the dragon considering her offer.

"Who is this?" He asked.

"I'm his servant." Belinda said without thinking.

The dragon went to her, Ezakiel wanted to protect her but all the dragon did was sniffing the treasure chest. Belinda trembled in fright.

"Fine, I'll let you enter the garden. The treasure chest must stay in this cave." Belinda put the chest down and run off to Ezakiel's side. Her hands were sweaty when she held his hands.

The dragon moved to the side to make way for them. He just watched them enter the gate without looking back. Once they disappeared into the garden, the dragon decided to continue sleeping.

Once they got past the dragon, they entered the garden that stood before them.

The gate opened automatically. What lay before their eyes were something so beautiful and it brought serenity to their soul. Everything that Ezakiel had once believed as a myth had become a reality. The mermaids, goblins, pixies, the dragon and now this.

There was a tall fountain in the middle of it. The water was so crystal clear. Flower petals were floating on top of the water which made it look stunning.

Ezakiel scanned the area for the butterfly fairy but he could see nothing. The garden was full of roses everywhere in many kinds of colors; red, yellow and mostly pink. The air seemed to be filled with its scent.

Belinda walked slowly towards the roses that were beside her, she had never seen roses before and the red one caught her interest. She brought her nose close to the red rose and smelt it. She did not realize that something was wrapping around her legs and hands. Once she realized it, the thorns had already sliced her skin painfully. Belinda yelled out Ezakiel's name.

Ezakiel saw it and quickly came to her aid and took the dagger from her to cut the roots. Tears were already trailing down her cheek but he still could not get the roots away from her. The roots were being controlled by someone and she could only be freed if the one who was controlling the roots did it.

"You can't save her." A voice suddenly came from behind. He turned only to face the butterfly fairy that looked furious to see them in her garden. Her wings were far bigger than the pixies', and her hair was long and curly. The small roses on top of her head formed something that looked like a crown.

"Please, let her go." Ezakiel begged her. "If I let her go, you will tell me exactly why you trespassed my garden." She said.

"Yes."

The butterfly fairy motioned her hands until the roots slowly unclasped Belinda. Her hands had scratches because of the thorn. The fairy came towards her and healed the wounds on her. The glitters that came out of her hands made the pain go away and she felt relieved.

"Now speak." She faced Ezakiel as soon she was done with Belinda.

"We're here to find the Forbidden Rose for my Queen Rose. She is sick because of the curse that has been put by her uncle. My kingdom and the people need her; she gives us hope to fight. She does not deserve to suffer in the hands of his evil uncle. I came here because she makes me believe in the myth of the Forbidden Rose and its healing power." He held Belinda's hand while he spoke.

"I know you are the fairy who guards the Rose. I'm not a bad person. My intention is pure." The fairy saw honesty in him, but, she had guarded the rose for centuries. The rose was made from the blood of the moon goddess. It was made for people who were in great need but the evil always wanted it to gain more power. That was the reason she had never allowed strangers in her garden, but these two humans were different. "If that is what you seek, I want you to answer my riddle." She said.

"Alright." Ezakiel said. He was all ready for it.

"Blink is the key, to bring darkness and light together. It is dark when it closes; it is bright when it opens?" At first Ezakiel could not figure out the answer. It could probably be a thing but the riddle she had given him was a tricky one. But, he figure it out eventually.

"Eyelashes." He said. The fairy did not look surprised; she got the feeling that he would know the answer. The riddle was only to test his earnestness to have the Forbidden Rose that she had guarded so faithfully in her garden.

"You are right," The fairy held her palm out to reveal a big blue velvet rose to him. Ezakiel was so happy that the fairy was eventually willing to give him what he really wanted by the end of this quest. "I present this to you, not just because you have answered my riddle but also because of your pure heart." The Rose was now on his palm. It felt so warm and soft with the petals against his skin.

Ezakiel Adventure To Enchanted Forest

"Thank you." He said.

"You and your Queen deserve it. Let me send you back to your world." They nodded in agreement.

The fairy made rain glitters on them, until slowly the wind carried their bodies away and disappeared from her garden. When they were gone, the butterfly fairy decided to move her garden away from the cave to someplace elsewhere so she would not be interrupted by any strangers. She had done her duty and now she needed to move on with her life.

A week after the quest, Queen Rose had finally recovered from the curse with the blue velvet rose that Ezakiel had fetched in his quest. He told her everything that he had gone through during the quest. Queen Rose was pleased that she could see him marry to the beautiful woman name Belinda. Their parents agreed with their reunion.

Queen Rose stepped down from her throne and relinquished her reign as the Queen of Gardenia. She passed it to Ezakiel. Ezakiel refused to accept the throne at first because he was just a knight. Queen Rose persisted so she gathered the people of the kingdom and asked if they were agreeable to the idea of Ezakiel taking over the throne.

Needless to say, it was a unanimous consensus and without further argument, Ezakiel and his new bride, Belinda, became the king and queen of the Kingdom of Gardenia. King Arganold who heard the news was suddenly frightened with the new king. Ezakiel had strong acquaintances that were the enemies of King Arganold. So he did not dare to fight him and bring destruction in his lands.

In the end, Ezakiel took his lovely wife to live in the castle and Queen Rose moved to another castle that had the view of the blue sea. He was happy with his life and vowed that he would protect the land and his family from enemies. He hoped that his love for Belinda could take them to the stairway of heaven.

- THE END -

Ann

Dear Reader,

The beginning is always a mess, you stumble, fail and made bad decisions. But…it's part of the lessons in life. I have to admit…this book was a direct result of so many bad decisions in the past and my insecurities.

Writing is much more than a hobby; it is a passion that if I simply just ignore it I will feel like a part of me is not complete. To *you* that read this special letter, if you have set goals for yourself, go and get it, it is not a sin to take one step at a time. If you feel like people do not support you well enough or just don't believe you will reach it. Hey! Look at me…I don't even believe in myself that I had come this far.

Your goals depend on your hard work and commitment. Without those two…trust me you will achieve nothing.

With warmest regards,
Ann Ally

Lightning Source UK Ltd.
Milton Keynes UK
UKHW051255220820
368606UK00030B/960